D0599191

I'm Your Bus

by
Marilyn Singer

pictures by
Evan Polenghi

SCHOLASTIC INC.
New York Toronto London Auckland
Sydney Mexico City New Delhi Hong Kong

Many thanks to my fabulous editor, Andrea Davis Pinkney, and the swell folks at Scholastic, and to my always-helpful husband, Steve Aronson. —M.S.

Special thanks to Andrea Davis Pinkney and Marijka Kostiw for driving this bus with grace and style. And an extra-special *beep* of gratitude to Barbara Greenberg for bringing all of us together. —E.P.

No part of this publication may be reproduced, stored in a retrieval system, or transmitted in any form or by any means, electronic, mechanical, photocopying, recording, or otherwise, without written permission of the publisher.
For information regarding permission, write to Scholastic Inc., Attention: Permissions Department, 557 Broadway, New York, NY 10012.

ISBN-13: 978-0-545-08919-7
ISBN-10: 0-545-08919-0

Copyright © 2009 by Marilyn Singer.
Illustrations copyright © 2009 by Evan Polenghi.
All rights reserved. Published by Scholastic Inc.
SCHOLASTIC and associated logos are trademarks and/or registered trademarks of Scholastic Inc.

12 11 10 9 8 7 6 5 4 3 2 1 9 10 11 12 13 14/0

Printed in the U.S.A. 08

This edition first printing, September 2009

The text type was set in Gill Sans Bold.
The display type was set in F 2 F Tagliatelle Sugo, and Chancy DeluxxeBold.
The illustrations in this book were done in digital media.
Book design by Marijka Kostiw

To Andrew and Mary —M.S.

To my nephews,

Ethan & Julian Quinn —E.P.

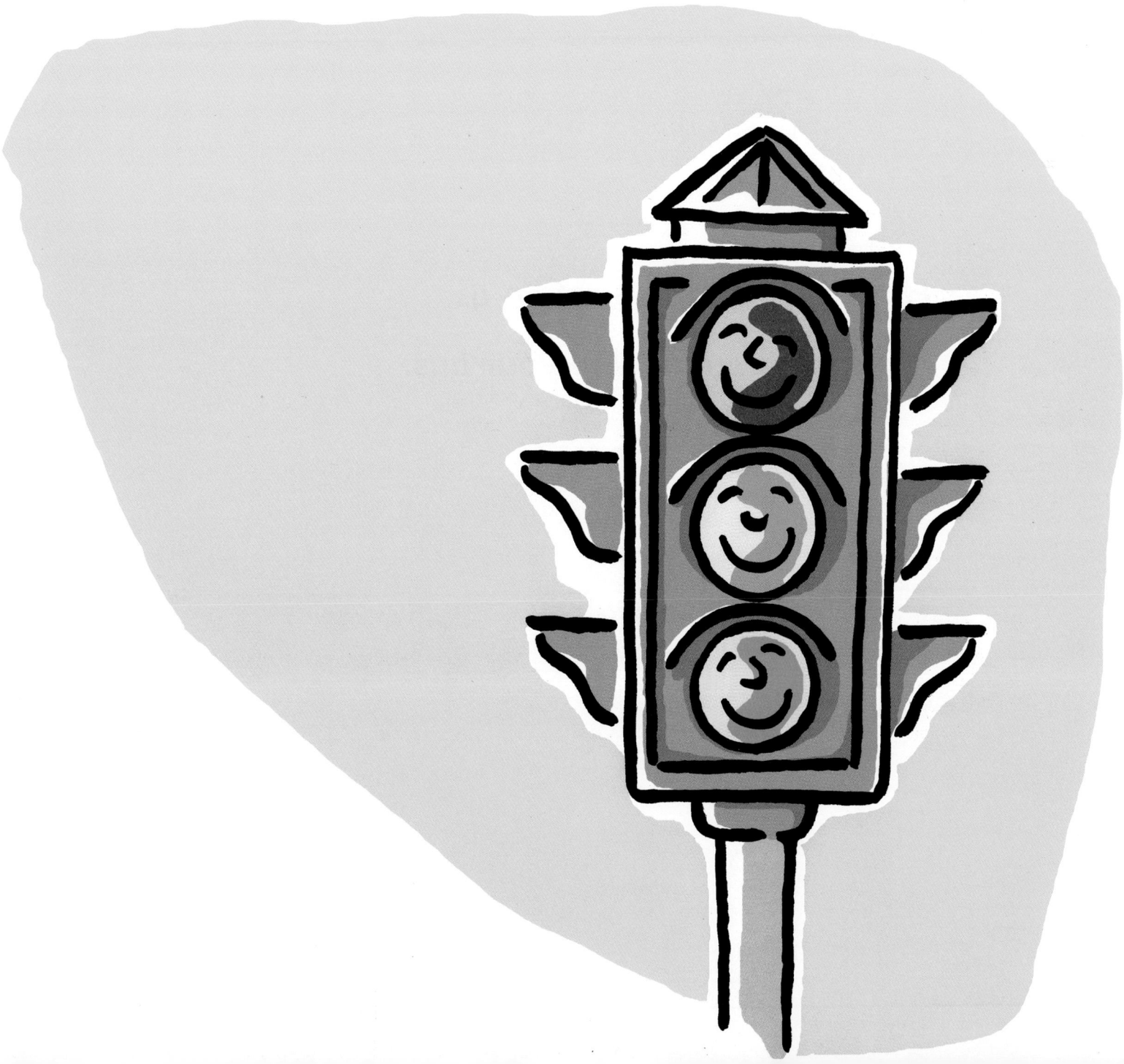

Howdy, you can count on us.

Morning, evening, I'm your bus.

HELLO!
STOP

Sweepers sweeping, bakers baking.

Dawn is barely even breaking.

Time for buses to be waking!

WAKE UP!
SCHOOL BUS
SCHOOL BUS
SCHOOL BUS
SCHOOL BUS
SCHOOL BUS

Hurry, hurry, now it's eight!

Busy buses can't be late.

In the morning we won't wait!

Get on, Jamie, Carlos, Gus,

Casey, Lacey. I'm your bus.

HURRY!

TOM'S TIRES
TIRES
SCHOOL BUS
SCHOOL BUS
SCHOOL BUS

Past the waving traffic cop.

Past the friendly tire shop.

There's the school zone.

Buses, stop!

Watch those backpacks coming through.

Have fun today. Learn something new.

Later we'll come back for you.

Hailey, Michael, Hannah, Russ,

see you later. I'm your bus.

HAVE A NICE DAY!

On the seats, we buses find

lots of schoolbooks—every kind—

pencils, glasses left behind.

Bats and caps—how fabulous!

I'll keep them safe 'cause I'm your bus.

SCIENCE
MATH
STORIES

Buses may take you to see

a zoo, a farm, a factory.

We linger outside patiently.

BEEP!
BOOKS &
SCHOOL SUPPLIES
TAXI
TAXI

Taxis zip by on their way
to an airport or café.
Buses go home, sit, and stay.

Quiet hours, we don't fuss.
Parking, driving, I'm your bus.

Yay! The school day's at an end.

Kids are leaving. They depend on each bus to be a friend.

Buses lined up in a row.

Lisa, Devin, Chloe, Mo,

find your bus and off you'll go!

How'd you grade me? Wow, A+!

I'm so proud that I'm your bus.

A+

Night is falling. Watchmen guard.

Buses settled in the yard.

We had fun and we worked hard.

SCHOOL BUS
SCHOOL BUS
SCHOOL BUS
SCHOOL BUS
SCHOOL BUS

Through the city, limos creep.

Shhh, don't toot, don't honk, don't beep.

Tired buses are asleep.

ZZZZ

Tomorrow you can count on us.

Daytime, nighttime, I'm your bus.

NEW DAY!